CLASSIC TALES OF
BABAR

CLASSIC TALES OF
BABAR

JEAN DE BRUNHOFF

HERITAGE

EGMONT

HERITAGE

EGMONT

First published in Great Britain by Egmont UK Limited
The Yellow Building, 1 Nicholas Road, London W11 4AN

ISBN 978 1 4052 6420 4

1 3 5 7 9 10 8 6 4 2

A CIP catalogue record for this title is available from the British Library

Printed and bound in Italy

51086/1

EGMONT LUCKY COIN

Our story began over a century ago, when seventeen-year-old Egmont Harald Petersen found a coin in the street.

He was on his way to buy a flyswatter, a small hand-operated printing machine that he then set up in his tiny apartment.

The coin brought him such good luck that today Egmont has offices in over 30 countries around the world. And that lucky coin is still kept at the company's head offices in Denmark.

FOREWORD

In his distinctive green suit and golden crown, Babar the Elephant is immediately one of the most recognisable characters in children's literature. As with many well-loved classics, he was first created by Jean de Brunhoff and his wife to entertain their young son.

In the 1930s, de Brunhoff began to develop and set these stories down on paper. At about the same time, he was diagnosed with tuberculosis and it may have been this, at the dawn of the creative process, which made him determined not to shy away from tragedy in his stories. In the opening pages of *The Story of Babar the Little Elephant*, Babar's mother is shot and killed by 'a cruel hunter'. This may seem like rather a bleak beginning for a children's book, but the power of these stories lies in their seamless combination of serious themes and great humour.

Although the stories themselves are flawlessly and charmingly told (and unusually presented in handwritten-style type) it is the superb illustrations that brought them such great acclaim and ensured their longevity. De Brunhoff studied painting at the Academie de la Grand Chaumiere in Montparnasse, and his skill is evident. The illustration alone almost tells each story, and the bold yet sensitive palette, vast panoramas and minute detailing set a benchmark in the emerging picture book genre.

The first story to be published was *The Story of Babar the Little Elephant*. Six more followed, *Babar and his Children* and *Babar and Father Christmas* being published posthumously. The first story was published in English in 1934, with a well-known foreword by A. A. Milne in which he proclaimed, 'I salute Monsieur de Brunhoff. I am at his feet'. Since then, millions of Babar books have been sold all around the world. Jean de Brunhoff's work has inspired TV series, films, classical music and a huge range of merchandising.

Almost a decade after his father's death, de Brunhoff's son Laurent decided to continue the Babar series and the books took a more educational direction. However it is his father's works that remain the most enduring, two of which, *The Story of Babar* and *Babar the King,* are published in this Egmont Heritage edition.

CONTENTS

JEAN DE BRUNHOFF

THE STORY
OF
BABAR

the little elephant

with a preface by A.A. Milne

HERITAGE

EGMONT

Preface

Two years ago at a friend's house I was introduced to Babar and Celeste. They spoke French then but they spoke it with a charming simplicity which saved me from all embarrassment. With a little trouble I managed to get them into my own house; and with no trouble at all they settled down at once as part of the family.

Since then I have been insisting that my publishers should take out naturalisation papers for them, and let them settle down at once in everybody else's family.

So here they are.

If you love elephants you will love Babar and Celeste. If you have never loved elephants you will love them now. If you who are grown-up have never been fascinated by a picture-book before, then this is the one which will fascinate you. If you who are a child do not take these enchanting people to your heart; if you do not spend delightful hours making sure that no detail of their adventures has escaped you; then you deserve to wear gloves and be kept off wet grass for the rest of your life.

I can say no more. I salute Monsieur de Brunhoff. I am at his feet.

A. A. Milne

In the Great Forest
a little elephant was born.
His name was Babar.
His mother loved him dearly
and used to rock him to sleep
with her trunk,
singing to him softly the while.

Babar grew fast.
Soon he was playing with the other baby elephants.

He was one of the nicest of them.
Look at him digging in the sand with a shell.

One day Babar was having
a lovely ride on his mother's back,
when a cruel hunter,
hiding behind a bush,
shot at them.

He killed Babar's mother.
The monkey hid himself, the birds flew away,
and Babar burst into tears.
The hunter ran up
to catch poor Babar.

Babar was very frightened
and ran away
from the hunter.
After some days,
tired and footsore,
he came to a town.

He was amazed,
for it was
the first time
he had ever seen
so many houses.

What strange things he saw!
Beautiful avenues!
Motorcars and motorbuses!
But what interested Babar
most of all was
two gentlemen
he met in the street.

He thought to himself:
"What lovely clothes they have got!
I wish I could
have some too!
But how can I get them?"

Luckily he was seen by
a very rich old lady
who understood
little elephants,
and knew at once
that he was longing for
a smart suit.
She loved making others happy,
so she gave him
her purse.

"Thank you, Madam,"
said Babar.

Without wasting a moment
Babar went into a big shop.
He got into the lift.
It was such fun
going up and down
in this jolly little box,
that he went ten times to the very top
and ten times down again to the bottom.
He was going up once more
when the lift-boy said to him:
"Sir, this is not a toy.
You must get out now
and buy
what you want.
Look, here is
the shop-walker."

a shirt,
collar
and
tie,

a suit
of a
delightful
green
colour,

bought:

next
a lovely
bowler
hat,

and
finally
shoes
and
spats.

25

Babar was so pleased
with his purchases
and satisfied
with his appearance
that he paid a visit
to the photographer.

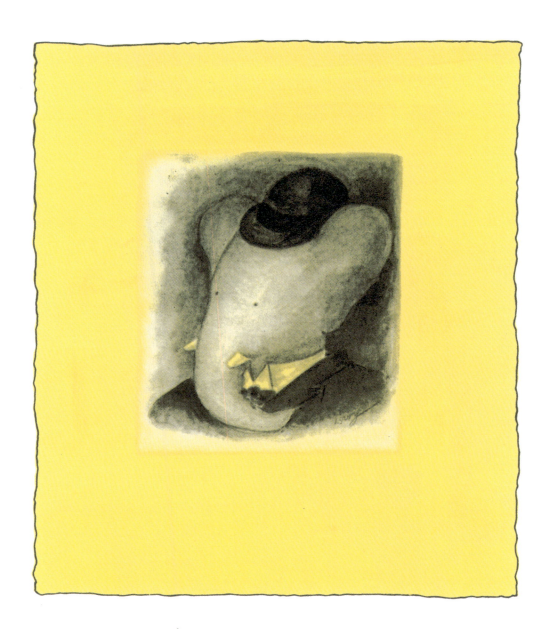

And here is his photograph.

Babar went to dinner
with his friend the Old Lady.
She, too, thought he looked very smart
in his new suit.
After dinner, he was so tired
that he went early to sleep.

Babar made his home
in the Old Lady's house.
Every morning
they did their exercises together,
and then Babar had
his bath.

Every day he drove out in the car
that the Old Lady had bought him.
She gave him everything that he wanted.

A learned professor gave him lessons.
Babar was very attentive,
and always gave the right answer.
He was a most promising pupil.

In the evenings, after dinner,
he told the Old Lady's friends
all about his life in the Great Forest.

And yet
Babar was not altogether happy:
he could no longer play about
in the Great Forest
with his little cousins
and his friends the monkeys.
He often gazed
out of the window,
dreaming of his childhood,
and when he thought
of his dear mother
he used to cry.

Two years passed by.
One day he was out for a walk,
when he met two little elephants
with no clothes on.
"Why, here are Arthur and Celeste,
my two little cousins!"
he cried in amazement to the Old Lady.

Babar hugged Arthur and Celeste
and took them to buy some lovely clothes.

Next, he took them to a tea-shop,
where they had some delicious cakes.

Meanwhile in the Great Forest
all the elephants were searching
for Arthur and Celeste
and their mothers grew more and more anxious.

Luckily, an old bird
flying over the town
had spied them,
and hurried back to tell the elephants.

The mothers went to the town
to fetch Arthur and Celeste.
They were very glad when they found them,
but they scolded them all the same
for having run away.

Babar made up his mind
to return to the Great Forest
with Arthur and Celeste and their mothers.
The Old Lady
helped him to pack.

When everything was ready for the journey
Babar kissed his old friend good-bye.
If he had not been so sorry to leave her
he would have been delighted to go home.
He promised to come back to her,
and never to forget her.

Off they went!
There was no room
for the mother elephants
in the car.
So they ran behind,
lifting up their trunks
so as not to breathe in
the dust.
The Old Lady
was left alone,
sadly thinking:
"When shall I see my little Babar again?"

Alas! That very day the King of the elephants
had eaten a bad mushroom.

It had poisoned him. He had been very ill,
and then had died.
It was a terrible misfortune.

After his funeral
the oldest elephants met together
to choose a new King.

Just at that moment they heard a noise and turned round.
What a wonderful sight they saw!
It was Babar arriving in his car,
with all the elephants running and shouting:
"Here they are! Here they are!
They have come back!
Hullo, Babar! Hullo, Arthur!
Hullo, Celeste!
What lovely clothes!
What a beautiful car!"

Then Cornelius,
the oldest elephant of all,
said, in his quavering voice:
"My dear friends, we must have a new King.
Why not choose Babar?
He has come back from the town,
where he has lived among men and learnt much.
Let us offer him the crown."
All the elephants thought
that Cornelius had spoken wisely,
and they listened eagerly
to hear what Babar would say.

"I thank you all,"
said Babar;
"But before accepting the crown
I must tell you
that on our journey in the car
Celeste and I
got engaged to be married.
If I become your King, she will be your Queen."

"Long live Queen Celeste!
Long live King Babar!!"
the elephants shouted with one voice.
And that was how Babar became King.

"Cornelius," said Babar,
"you have such good ideas
that I shall make you a general,
and when I get my crown
I will give you my hat.
In a week's time
I am going to marry Celeste.
We will give a grand party
to celebrate our marriage
and our coronation."
And Babar asked the birds
to take invitations to all the animals,

and he told the dromedary to go to the town
to buy him some fine wedding clothes.

The guests began to arrive.
The dromedary brought the clothes
just in time for the ceremony.

After the wedding and the coronation

everyone danced merrily.

The party was over.
Night fell,
and the stars came out.
The hearts of
King Babar and Queen Celeste
were filled with happy dreams.

Then all the world slept.
The guests had gone home,
very pleased and very tired
after dancing so much.
For many a long day
they will remember that wonderful ball.

Then King Babar and Queen Celeste
set out on their honeymoon,
in a glorious yellow balloon,
to meet with new adventures.

THE END

JEAN DE BRUNHOFF

BABAR
THE KING

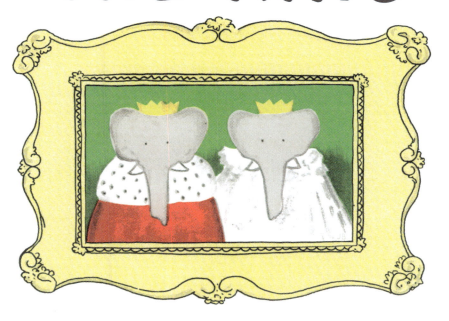

King Babar and Queen Celeste
led a happy life
in the country of the elephants.
Peace had been signed with the rhinoceroses.
Their friend, the Old Lady,
had gladly agreed to stay with them.
She often told stories to the elephant children,
and her little monkey, Zephir,
sat up in a tree and listened too.

Leaving the Old Lady with Queen Celeste, Babar
went for a walk along the shores of the big lake
with Cornelius, the oldest and wisest
of the elephants, and said to him:
"This place is so beautiful that every morning
when I wake up,

I should like to see it.
We must build our town here.
Our houses will be by the water
in the midst of flowers and birds."
Zephir, who was with them,
was trying to catch a butterfly.

While chasing the butterfly
Zephir met his friend, Arthur,
the little cousin of the King and Queen,
who was enjoying himself, looking for snails.
Suddenly they saw
one, two, three, four dromedaries,
five, six, seven dromedaries,
eight, nine, ten . . .
so many that they could no longer count them.
"Will you please tell us where King Babar is?"
said the leader of the dromedaries.

Arthur and Zephir
led the dromedaries to Babar.
They had brought his heavy luggage
and all the things he had bought
when on his honeymoon abroad.
Babar said, "Thank you, dromedaries.
You must be tired: rest for a while
in the shade of the palm trees."
Then, turning to the Old Lady
and Cornelius, he added,
"Now we shall be able
to build our town."

Having called a meeting of the elephants,
Babar stood on a box, and
in a loud voice spoke these words:
"My friends, in these trunks and bales and cases
I have presents for all of you —
dresses, hats, silks, paint-boxes, drums,
tins of peaches, feathers, racquets,
and many other things.
I will give them to you
as soon as we have built our new town.
This town, the town of the elephants,
I propose that we call Celesteville
in honour of your Queen."
"Hear! Hear!"
cried all the elephants,
raising their trunks in the air.

The elephants set to work at once.
Arthur and Zephir distributed the tools, and
Babar showed each one the work he had to do.
He drew plans of the streets and houses;
he ordered one party to cut down trees,
another to carry stones,
and others again to saw wood and to dig foundations.
How eagerly they all set to work!
The Old Lady put on the gramophone.
Babar played the trumpet
now and again, for a change;
like all elephants he loved music.
Thoroughly enjoying themselves,
they hammered, and pulled, and pushed,
and dug, and tossed, and carried,
flapping their great ears the while.

In the great lake
The fishes grumbled to each other.
"We can no longer sleep in peace,"
they said,
"those elephants make too much noise!
What can they be doing?
When we jump out of the water
we have no time to see anything properly.
We must ask
the frogs."

The birds, too, met together
to talk about the elephants:
the pelicans and flamingos,
the ducks and the ibises, and even the tiniest ones.
They twittered and chirped and sang,
and the parrots grew enthusiastic,
repeating over and over again:
"Come and see Celesteville, most beautiful of towns!
Come and see Celesteville, most beautiful of towns!"

Behold Celesteville! The elephants have just
finished building it, and are now resting or bathing.
Babar, with Arthur and Zephir, is sailing round
it in his boat, admiring his new Capital.
Each elephant has
a house of his own.

The Old Lady's house is at the top on the left
and Babar's at the top on the right.
All the windows look out
over the big lake.
The Palace of Work is next to the Palace
of Pleasure, which is very convenient.

Babar now kept his promise:
to each elephant he gave a present,
together with good working-clothes
and lovely holiday-costumes.
When they had thanked their King
the elephants went dancing home.

Babar arranged that on the following Sunday,
after dressing up in their best,
the elephants should have a Garden Party
in the grounds of the Palace of Pleasure.
So the gardeners had plenty to do,
raking the paths, watering the flowers,
and planting out the beds.

The little elephants planned a surprise
for Babar and Celeste.
They asked Cornelius
to teach them
the song of the elephants.
It was Arthur's idea.
They practised hard
to get it perfect by Sunday!

SONG OF THE ELEPHANTS

MELODY

Pa-ta- li di - ra-pa-ta crom-da crom-da ri-pa-lo

REFRAIN:

Pa-ta   Pa-ta   Ko Ko   Ko- - - - - - - - - - - -

WORDS

1ST VERSE

PATALI DIRAPATA
CROMDA CROMDA RIPALO
PATA PATA
KO KO KO

2ND VERSE

BOKORO DIPOULITO
RONDI RONDI PEPINO
PATA PATA
KO KO KO

3RD VERSE

ÉMANA KARASSOLI
LOUCRA LOUCRA PONPONTO
PATA PATA
KO KO KO

NOTE: This song is the old chant of the Mammoths,
Cornelius himself doesn't know what the words mean —

The cooks set to work with all speed
to prepare cakes and pastries of every kind.
Queen Celeste helped them.
Zephir tasted the vanilla cream
to see if it was sweet enough.
He dipped his finger in it,
then his hand, then his arm.
Arthur longed to plunge in his trunk.

For one last taste
Zephir leaned over and put out his tongue,
and, plop! in he fell.
The head cook was very angry,
and fished Zephir out by the tail.
Poor Zephir was a dreadful sight,
yellow and slimy.
Celeste took him away to wash him.

Sunday came at last. In the gardens
of the Palace of Pleasure the elephants
walked about dressed in their best. The children
sang their song and Babar kissed them all.

The refreshments were delicious. What a glorious day.
The time passed only too quickly!
And here you see the Old Lady
arranging the last game of hide and seek.

The next day
after their morning bathe in the lake,
the elephant children went to school.
They were always happy to see
their dear mistress, the Old Lady.
Their lessons with her were
never dull.

When she had set the little ones to work,
she taught the bigger ones. "What is
three times three?" "Eight," said Arthur.
"No, nine," said Ottilie, who sat next to him.
"Nine: a cat-o'-nine-tails," shouted Zephir.
"Nine," echoed Arthur.
"I will not forget that again."

The elephants who were too old to go to school
each chose a profession or trade.
For example: Tapitor was a shoemaker,
Pilophage an officer, Capoulosse a doctor,
Barbacol a tailor, Podular a sculptor, and Hatchibombotar
swept and watered the roads.
Doulamor was a musician, Olur a mechanic,
Poutifour a farmer, Fandago a scholar,
Justinien a painter and Coco a clown.
When Capoulosse had holes in his shoes
he took them to Tapitor, and
when Tapitor was ill Capoulosse attended him.
If Barbacol wanted to put a statuette
on his mantel-piece he told Podular,
and when Podular's jacket was worn out
Barbacol measured him for a new one.
Justinien painted Pilophage's portrait,
and Pilophage defended him against his enemies.
Hatchibombotar kept the streets tidy,
Olur repaired motorcars,
and, when they were tired, Doulamor played to them.
After solving difficult problems,
Fandago ate fruit grown by Poutifour.
As for Coco, he made them all laugh.

TAPITOR

CAPOULOSSE FANDAGO

BARBACOL

PODULAR

PILOPHAGE JUSTINIEN

DOULAMOR

POUTIFOUR

HATCHIBOMBOTAR OLUR

COCO

In Celesteville
the elephants work all the morning;
in the afternoon they do whatever they like.
They play, go for walks, read and dream.
Babar and Celeste loved a game of tennis
with Mr. and Mrs. Pilophage.

Cornelius, Fandago, Podular and Capoulosse
preferred to play boules.
The little elephants and Arthur and Zephir
enjoyed themselves with Coco, the clown.
There was also the pond for boats,
and they had many other games besides.

But what the elephants loved best of all

was the Theatre in the Palace of Pleasure.

The first thing every morning
Hatchibombotar watered the streets
with his motor watercart.
When Arthur and Zephir met him
they quickly took off their shoes,
and followed bare-foot.
"What a lovely shower-bath!"
they shouted.
One day, unfortunately,
Babar saw them:
"No dessert for you, you naughty children!"
he cried.

Like all little boys, Arthur and Zephir
were always up to mischief;
but they were not lazy.
At the Old Lady's house, Babar and Celeste
were astonished to hear them playing
the violin and 'cello.
"It's wonderful!" cried Celeste, and Babar said:
"Children, I am pleased with you.
Go to the cake-shop and choose whatever you like."

Arthur and Zephir enjoyed
eating the cakes,
but it gave them even more pleasure
to hear Cornelius read out,
on prize-giving day:
"First prize for music.
Equal, Arthur and Zephir."
They went back to their seats feeling very proud.
After he had given away the prizes
Cornelius made a very fine speech:

"And now, a happy holiday to you all!"
he cried, and sat down
amid loud cheers,
forgetting that his beautiful hat
lay on his chair.
He flattened it out completely.
"It's just like a pancake!" exclaimed Zephir.
Cornelius looked at it
in horror.
What was he to wear at the coming Fête?

The Old Lady promised Cornelius
to trim his old bowler with feathers,
and, to cheer him up, she invited him
for a ride in the beautiful roundabout
that had just been ordered by Babar.

Podular had carved the animals,
Justinien had painted them,
and the machinery had been put in by Olur.
They were all three very clever.

The King's mechanical horse
had also been made by them.
Olur greased it well, and the King mounted it
to give it a final trial
before the Grand Fête
to commemorate the anniversary
of the foundation of Celesteville.

In glorious weather the Grand Fête took place. At the head
of the procession marched Arthur and Zephir and the band.
Cornelius, wearing his retrimmed hat, followed;

then came the soldiers, and the arts and crafts guilds.
All the elephants who were not in the procession
watched the memorable pageant.

1

On his way home
after the Fête
Zephir saw
a strange-looking stick.

2

He stopped to pick it up.
Horror!
It was a snake
that rose with a hiss

3

and cruelly bit
the Old Lady
who had taken Zephir
in her arms.

4

Arthur hit out furiously
and broke his trumpet
on the serpent's back
and killed it.

The Old Lady,
with a swelling arm,
hastened
to the hospital.

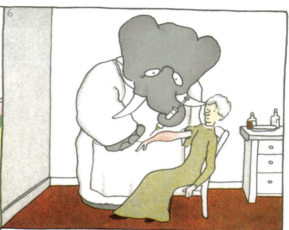

Dr. Capoulosse
attended her.
He at once injected
serum.

Feeling miserable,
Zephir sat
near his mistress
who was very ill.

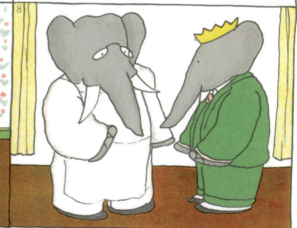

"I cannot tell
till tomorrow
whether she will recover,"
said the doctor to Babar.

On his way from the hospital
Babar heard cries of "Fire! Fire!"
Cornelius' house was in flames.
The staircase was already ablaze;
but, after many efforts, the firemen succeeded
in rescuing Cornelius by the window.
He was half-suffocated,
and injured by a falling beam.
Capoulosse was quickly called,
and gave him first aid
before removing him to hospital.
This terrible fire was caused by a lighted match
that Cornelius had thrown towards an ashtray;
but the match, still alight,
had fallen into the waste paper basket.

That night
when Babar went to bed,
he shut his eyes but could not sleep.
"What a dreadful day!" he thought.
"It began so well;
why did it finish so badly?
Before these two accidents
we were so happy and peaceful in Celesteville.

"We had forgotten what unhappiness was!
Oh, my old Cornelius,
and you, my dear old lady, my friend,
I would give my crown to see you both cured!
Capoulosse ought to telephone news of you.
How long this night seems, and how restless I am!"

At last Babar fell asleep.
He tossed and turned, and then dreamed.
He heard a knocking at his door,
Tap! Tap! Tap!
Then a voice said:
"It is I, Misfortune,
with some of my companions.
We have come to visit you."
He looked out of the window
and saw a hideous old woman,
surrounded by a crowd of ugly creatures.
As he opened his mouth to shout:
"Shoo! Off with you!"
he heard a sweet sound that made him pause, -
Frrr! Frrr! Frrr!
like the wings of birds in flight
and he saw coming towards him . . .

. . . glorious elephants with wings,
who chased Misfortune
far from Celesteville,
and brought with them
Happiness.
At that moment Babar awoke
and felt better.

GOODNESS

FEAR

DESPAIR

SLOTH

MISFORTUNE

DISEASE

ANGER

STUPIDITY

DISCOURAGEMENT

Babar dressed and hastened to the hospital.
Oh, Joy! What did he see?
His two dear invalids
walking in the garden.
He could hardly believe his eyes.
"I have quite recovered,"
said Cornelius,
"but all this excitement
has made me feel as hungry as a hunter.
Come and have breakfast,
and after that we will rebuild my house."

EGMONT PRESS: ETHICAL PUBLISHING

Egmont Press is about turning writers into successful authors and children into passionate readers – producing books that enrich and entertain. As a responsible children's publisher, we go even further, considering the world in which our consumers are growing up.

Safety First
Naturally, all of our books meet legal safety requirements. But we go further than this; every book with play value is tested to the highest standards – if it fails, it's back to the drawing-board.

Made Fairly
We are working to ensure that the workers involved in our supply chain – the people that make our books – are treated with fairness and respect.

Responsible Forestry
We are committed to ensuring all our papers come from environmentally and socially responsible forest sources.

For more information, please visit our website at www.egmont.co.uk/ethical